What if?

For my inspiring children — JS

For my brother and Vania — BN

First published in 1999 by Macmillan Children's Books
a division of Macmillan Publishers Limited
25 Eccleston Place, London SW1W 9NF
and Basingstoke
Associated companies worldwide

ISBN 0 333 73485 8 (HB)
ISBN 0 333 73486 6 (PB)

1 3 5 7 9 8 6 4 2

A CIP catalogue record for this book is available
from the British Library

Printed in Belgium

What if?

Jonathan Shipton

Illustrated by
Barbara Nascimbeni

Macmillan Children's Books

What if . . .
it stopped raining?

What if it stopped raining,
and you went outside,
and down behind the
shed you found . . .

. . . a sunflower as tall as a skyscraper!

What if you
were really good
at climbing and
up you went, fast
as a monkey,

hands and feet,
leaf by leaf,

until you were as high as
the highest chimneypot!

What if you carried
on until you were
higher than a bird
can fly . . .

... until your head burst through the clouds!

What if there's a girl there?

(And you're not sure you like girls . . .)

But this girl is BRILLIANT!

She's called Arabella
and she knows how
to bounce on clouds.

She springs and spins inside out and upside down

and round and about.

And you've never had so much fun, ever!

Then what if
Arabella says she
knows where storms are made . . .
and she takes you there to where
the lightning flashes and
the dark clouds rumble over
the mountains to the sea.

What if you say you're
a little bit frightened.

But Arabella says
it's an adventure!
But what if you got
Really Soaking Wet!

And Arabella had to take
you off to the desert to dry your
clothes, and the drips fell on the camels.

Then it got hotter . . .
and
hotter . . .
and
hotter . . .

... and suddenly your cloud starts to melt away ...

So you head for home as quickly
as you can, and Arabella
shows you how to

wave your arms to go faster!

And just in time
you screech to a
stop, and there's
your sunflower,
popping its
yellow head
through the
clouds.

But what if it's a long, long way off, and you're too scared to jump . . . But Arabella says "You can do it! You can do ANYTHING if you try!"

So you jump.
And it's the
best jump
you've
ever
done!

And as you fly through the air you can hear
Arabella clapping and cheering.

Down you go,
leaf by leaf,
like a little monkey.

Down
and
down
and
down,
all the way
down to the
Good Solid
Ground.

But what if you
landed on a
secret door . . .